The
Perils of
Quadrant X

The Perils of Quadrant X

NANCY KRULIK

SCHOLASTIC INC.
New York Toronto London Auckland Sydney

ISBN 0-590-18940-9

12 11 10 9 8 7 6 5 4 3 2 1   8 9/9 0 1 2 3/0

Printed in the U.S.A.

First Scholastic printing, September 1998

The Perils of Quadrant X

1
Storm!

There were three things ten-year-old Will Robinson missed most of all when he stopped to think about it. The first was the Houston Astros, his hometown baseball team. The second was new music by Replicated Eugenics, his favorite cloned rock band. The third was a good handful of Chocolate Nutrinos, the only nutritionally balanced candy worth poring over computer data with.

Well, the Astros were billions of uncharted light-years away back home on Earth. It was probably still a miracle for them to even get close to the pennant. And although he had brought along his collection of classic Replicated Eugenics holo-music, Will knew it would be some time before he could hear anything new by his favorite group. He just hoped the band wouldn't break up before he and his family found their way back home. As for Chocolate Nutrinos, he had to admit his mom was able to whip up a pretty good imitation — even if she sometimes did go a little heavy on the protein powder.

"Will, get up here and help me with the hydroponic garden!" came an angry voice over the cabin loudspeaker.

Will groaned. It was his sister Penny. He had finally been able to lock himself away in his cabin long enough to log in a series of new computer simulated star-charts he had been wanting to plot, when Penny's call interrupted him. She was in the solarium tending to the garden that helped supply the ship with its abundance of fresh fruits and vegetables. Will had been scheduled to join her up there, but lost track of time. Gardening was not his favorite shipboard chore. Besides, he wanted to see what kind of star mapping he could do before the ship's next leap into hyperdrive, which was less than an hour away.

Hyperdrive leaps were regularly scheduled now. Without his father's miraculous invention of a hyperdrive interface, Will and his family stood little chance of ever getting back home. With hyperdrive, the *Jupiter 2* could leap billions of light-years across space, a distance it would normally take several lifetimes to travel.

There was only one problem. Despite all their know-how, it was impossible for his father and Major West to calculate the exact part of space a hyperdrive leap would take them. Half the time they didn't know if they were getting closer to home — or farther away.

That was why Will began spending long hours in his cabin testing star map simulations — simulations he felt could create a map that would take them home. To Will, each map was a marker of where they had been. By randomly inputting an infinite number of these "markers" into his computer, Will hoped to be able to help his dad and Major West plot a reasonable hyperdrive leap, one that might take them home. It was a long shot, he knew, but Will wanted to do everything he could to speed up getting back home: back to baseball, rock 'n' roll, and real store-bought Chocolate Nutrinos.

"Will," came Penny's agitated voice again. "Answer me or I'm telling Mom!"

Will had just scooped up a handful of imitation Nutrinos and was about to write a new star configuration when his intercom signaled again. He begrudgingly pressed the reply button next to his computer.

"You don't have to go supernova, sis," he replied with irritation. "I heard you the first time. I'll be right up."

Will entered the save command on his computer and logged off. Star-charting simulations would have to wait. He grabbed a pair of soil-stained gardening gloves and headed topside.

He found Penny in the solarium, which was situated at the uppermost level of the *Jupiter 2*, the huge saucer-shaped intergalactic spaceship that was now home to Will and his family. The solarium was a room that was covered by a clear, domed ceiling made out of an indestructible polymer that resisted any kind of deterioration from the forces of outer space. This allowed the *Jupiter 2*'s vast collection of plants, flowers, and foods to grow not only with the aid of the ship's artificial solar light, but with new light harnessed from the stars themselves.

"It's about time," said Penny, upon seeing her brother climb off the turbolift. "How do you expect us to maintain our food supply if we don't re-pot some of these oxygenating plants?"

Will could see by the smudges on her face and smock that his sister had already begun the messy process of re-potting. She ran a hand through her dark hair and sighed.

"How do you expect us to ever get home if I can't maintain

and update my star-chart simulation data base?" asked Will. "We're taking a leap in less than an hour, you know."

"Star-charting simulations? Is that what you were doing?" asked Penny. "I think Dad and Major West know enough in that department without needing your help."

"Dad and Don don't always have time for simulations before a leap," Will replied, offended. "And besides, they always appreciate any extra help I can give."

"What you do on your own time is your business, I guess," said Penny. "But on ship's time you're supposed to do ship's chores. And it's more likely we can grow a new patch of tomatoes than stumble on a simulated star map that'll take us home."

Will smirked. "That's just the kind of thing they must have told Galileo when he discovered there were stars in the Milky Way. Fortunately, he didn't listen."

"Your sister is correct, Will Robinson," a mechanical voice was heard approaching from the other end of the solarium. It was the ship's Robot, its arms stacked with empty potting trays. "The chances of successfully replenishing the solarium's tomato reserve is exactly one in ten in favor of. The odds of discovering a course back to Earth through computer simulation is one in one hundred nine trillion seven hundred three billion ten thousand nine million —"

"All right, Robot," interrupted Will. "I get the point. Hand over some trays."

The Robot extended the stack of trays. When Will reached for the top tray, the Robot's domed head snapped to alertness.

"Danger! Danger!" cried the Robot. "Cosmic storm approaching the ship!"

Will and Penny glanced through the huge solarium window. From deep within the vast alien starfield outside, a cluster of bright streaks were approaching. Very quickly the streaks grew in number. The Robot was right. They were cosmic lightning bolts, the kind caused by an electrical storm. There were hundreds, perhaps thousands of them. And they were heading right toward the ship at a terrifying speed!

2
Hyperdrive

"Those bolts are gonna hit us dead on!" shouted Will.

Sure enough, seconds later the ship was jolted by a powerful force from the impact of one of the lightning bolts. The force was so great that Will and Penny went rolling across the room, knocking over plants as they went. The Robot, unable to keep its balance, dropped the stack of potting trays and rolled away.

Will found himself thrown against a wall. He looked over and saw that Penny had fallen facedown and was covered by some fallen plants and dirt.

"Penny!" he shouted, running to his sister. "Are you all right?"

"I'm okay," replied Penny, shaking some dirt from her clothes. "Just a little dirty."

"Sensors indicate another impact is imminent!" announced the Robot. Then it extended its huge ball-bearinglike arms. "I suggest the two of you hold on to me. I can stabilize my weight and prevent the danger of any further injury from falling."

Will and Penny quickly grabbed the Robot's arms. Suddenly, the ship jerked again. Then again. Lightning bolts were now hitting the ship from all angles.

Will and Penny could see the bolts bouncing off the clear ceiling of the solarium. Luckily, the ceiling held strong, without the slightest crack from the impacts. But the barrage from the cosmic storm was so great that Will and Penny covered their faces in fear.

"Will! Penny! Are you all right?" came a familiar voice. Their mother, Maureen Robinson, had just arrived on the turbolift.

"We're okay, Mom," said Will as his mother made her way toward him unsteadily. She had to hold on to anything she could as the ship continually quaked each time it was struck by a lightning bolt.

"Mom, look out!" cried Penny. A shelf of potted plants had broken loose from the wall right above Mrs. Robinson's head. Mrs. Robinson rushed away from the wall just as the plants crashed to the floor.

"The children are safe as long as they hold on to me, Mrs. Robinson," said the Robot. "I suggest you do the same."

Mrs. Robinson joined Will and Penny and grabbed on to one of the Robot's arms.

"Maureen!" came a voice over the ship's main speakers. It was Will and Penny's father, Professor John Robinson. "Are the children all right?"

"We're fine, John," replied Mrs. Robinson. "Is everything ready at the con?"

"Don and I are about to initiate the hyperdrive sequence," said Professor Robinson. "Make sure you're holding on to something tight!"

"We're quite secure, dear," replied Mrs. Robinson. "Thanks to the Robot."

"Roger," acknowledged Professor Robinson. "Hyperdrive sequence beginning."

"But we weren't scheduled for the hyperdrive leap for another hour," remarked Will.

"The ship doesn't have enough power to pull away from the cosmic storm and our force shield doesn't have enough power to withstand this much impact," explained Mrs. Robinson. "Your father decided to step up the hyperdrive leap. It's the only way we can get to safety quickly."

"Hyperdrive? Now?" asked Penny, in a panic. "But what about Blawp!" She was worried about the unusual alien traveling companion she had rescued from another dimension.

"Blawp is okay, Penny," said Mrs. Robinson. "Judy and Dr. Smith made sure she was secured in a landing seat."

"But she won't understand what's going on," said Penny. "She'll be scared. I wish I could be with her."

Will rolled his eyes. "Don't be such a baby, Penny," he chided his sister. "If that lizard-monkey of yours is strapped in, she's probably better off than we are."

"That's not the point, Will, and you know it," Penny shot back. "I don't want her to be frightened."

"What's there to be frightened of?" laughed Will. "It's only a simple hyperdrive leap. Yeesh!"

"Stop arguing, both of you," interjected Mrs. Robinson. "And hold on tight to Robot."

"Hyperdrive countdown beginning," Professor Robinson announced. "Three . . . two . . . one . . . initiate!"

"Initiating hyperdrive," came another voice over the speaker. It was the ship's pilot, Major West.

Will listened carefully to the series of clicks and whirs that came over the loudspeaker from the control deck of the ship.

The sounds were being made as Major West initiated the hyperdrive. Will silently tested himself, trying to see if he could identify each sound by memory.

If Will's memory served him correctly, the next sound would be a low hum that would become louder and louder. That meant the hyperdrive leap was about to begin.

He was right.

"Everybody get ready!" he shouted with excitement as he grabbed tightly to the Robot's arm. "It's about to happen!"

"You are correct, Will Robinson," said the Robot. "Hyperdrive will begin in seconds."

The floors and walls began to vibrate. First the vibrations were slow, then they became very fast. Will looked at his mother and Penny. They, too, were vibrating at a terrific speed.

Will suddenly felt himself being hurled backward. He closed his eyes with anticipation. He had the sensation of being thrown across the room, but when he opened his eyes he saw that he and the others were still standing in the same spot clinging to the Robot. The only difference was everybody looked as if they were frozen in position.

Suddenly, everything — the walls, the tables, the shelves, and the plants — seemed to stretch around him. Things became distorted as if Will was looking at the spaceship through a hall of mirrors in an amusement park. He tried to speak, but when he did his voice came out slow and slurred.

Will looked up at the clear ceiling of the solarium. Through it he could see that the stars outside had begun to bend and stretch as well. Now the stars, as well as the lightning bolts that were attacking them, seemed like long, bright swirls across the outer space sky.

Next, Will saw that sections of the spaceship were beginning to disappear around him. And even though he could feel them, his mother, Penny, and the Robot disappeared as well.

Despite how he had taunted his sister just moments earlier, Will had to fight back the urge to panic. In his mind he knew that all these strange sights were the effects of the *Jupiter 2* entering hyperdrive space. He knew that the secret of hyperdrive was that it actually "warped" space — meaning it "bent" matter in such a way that allowed the *Jupiter 2* to travel great distances as if they were much shorter. In many ways, the sights Will saw were an optical illusion, a trick the hyperdrive effect played on his senses.

But in his heart, he was scared. And although he knew it would be over soon, he couldn't wait for the leap to finish.

When it was finally over there was no way Will could tell how long it had taken. It might have been minutes, it might have been hours, it might even have been just a few seconds. Hyperdrive, Will knew, distorted time as well as space. In any case, Will soon began to see his surroundings return to normal. The walls of the spaceship slowly began to reappear. His mother, Penny, and the Robot came back into view.

Through the solarium window Will could see the stars again. He noticed right away that the constellations were different, evidence that the leap had taken the *Jupiter 2* to some new location in outer space. Most important, however, the lightning bolts were gone. The ship and everyone aboard were safe.

"The hyperdrive transport is complete," announced the Robot. "I am destabilizing my bearings."

"Con to solarium," Will heard his father say over the speaker. "Maureen, is everybody okay?"

"We're fine, John," replied Mrs. Robinson. Will and Penny

were nodding in agreement as they released their grip on the Robot's arm. "Do you or Don have any idea where we are?"

"Negative," replied Major West. "I don't recognize a single constellation."

"The Electric Guitar!" Will suddenly exclaimed with excitement. He moved away from the Robot and was now looking out through the solarium window with a gaze of intense fascination.

"What was that, Will?" asked Professor Robinson.

Mrs. Robinson approached Will. She looked into the vast outer space sky trying to see what he was looking at. All she saw were millions of unfamiliar star clusters. "What are you looking at, Will?" she asked.

"That constellation out there," replied Will, pointing out at space. "I think I recognize it. In fact, I think it means we're closer to home than we've ever been before!"

3
Quadrant X

"Just before the cosmic storm, I was inputting some new entries into the star-chart simulation program in my computer," Will explained minutes later when the crew of the *Jupiter 2* had gathered on the control deck. "I'm certain that one of my entries matches that constellation out there."

Will's startling comment in the solarium — that he recognized a star constellation — had given everybody the hope that this latest hyperdrive leap had taken them closer to home. Now, they were gathered on the main deck to see if, indeed, Will's claim was true.

Will had transferred his star-chart simulation onto a microdisk and brought it with him. He handed it to Major West, who quickly placed it into the computer at his navigation station.

The navigation monitor came to life and displayed a series of electronic grids and graphs. Will's program was up and running. Soon images of star constellations took shape. Hundreds of different star groupings passed across the screen. Will made some entries into the computer. Finally, the screen settled on one constellation.

"There it is," said Will, locking in the image. "Star simulation number K-34 in Quadrant X. I named it the Electric Guitar because it kinda looks like one the Replicated Eugenics play."

"What a ridiculous name for a constellation," said Penny.

"What's wrong with it?" asked Will. "It's better than anything you could think up, lamebrain."

"I think it's a very creative name," said Judy, Will's oldest sister, as she watched the monitor with fascination. Judy was the *Jupiter 2*'s onboard physician.

"Who cares what the name is," said Dr. Smith. "Is it possible the boy may have stumbled onto something?"

"Anything is possible, Dr. Smith," said Professor Robinson. "Will, what makes you think that constellation out there is familiar? There's no constellation in our solar system that looks like it."

"Well, after I plotted the simulation I ran a standard inversion breakdown," said Will. "Look."

Will entered some more commands. Suddenly, the stars that made up the constellation on the monitor began to move and change their position. This happened twice.

"The computer found three possible inverted variations on the Electric Guitar," continued Will as the star images moved around. "The first two were unfamiliar. But the third is almost an identical match."

"Match for what?" asked his mother.

The constellation had changed again. This time a message flashed across the bottom of the computer screen that read:

PROBABLE DATA MATCH!
CONSTELLATION NAME: ELECTRIC GUITAR
CONSTELLATION MATCH: TAURUS THE BULL
MATCH PROBABILITY: NINETY-THREE PERCENT

13

"Yes, I can see it now!" exclaimed Dr. Smith, happily looking at the constellation through the ship's viewport. "It *is* Taurus! The constellation that's shaped like a bull! Will *was* right! We're home!"

"Dr. Smith, once again you have let your human emotions control your scientific logic," cautioned the Robot. "The probability that the constellation Will discovered in Quadrant X is Taurus the Bull is only at ninety-three percent. That still leaves a seven percent probability that he may be wrong."

"Check your calculations, tin-man," said Dr. Smith. "Anybody with a grade-schooler's knowledge of astronomy can see that we've entered familiar space!"

"The Robot's right, Dr. Smith," said Professor Robinson. "We'll have to run a few more tests before we can recalibrate our course."

"More tests would be a mere formality," said Smith. "I say we plot a course for that constellation without any further ado."

"Fortunately for us your vote carries little weight around here, Smith," said Major West as he input some commands into the computer. "I'm running a vector analysis now. It'll take some time, but the computer should be able to tell us if Will's Electric Guitar is a signpost toward home."

"Major West, whatever happened to that impulsive personality that you were so famous for back on Earth?" chided Dr. Smith. "Isn't it worth the risk to change our course despite the odds?"

"How about I stuff you into the space pod and jettison you toward that constellation all by yourself?" shot back Major West. "Would that be impulsive enough for you?"

"It would certainly be worth it if only for the pleasure of not having to share another minute of this aimless voyage with *you*," replied Smith without missing a beat.

"Oh, yeah?" replied Major West, turning red with anger and flexing his muscular arms, ready to fight. "Well, this voyage wouldn't be so 'aimless' if you hadn't tried to sabotage our mission and gotten us lost in space in the first place! And another thing: I'm sick and tired of your lazy, shiftless, good-for-nothing —"

"Warning! Warning!" the Robot suddenly interrupted. "Danger ahead! Danger ahead!"

"What is it, Robot?" asked Will.

"The *Jupiter 2* is headed for a high intensity energy field!" replied the Robot.

"Look!" shouted Penny, pointing at the viewport.

From out of the depths of space appeared a long, shimmering band of light that was getting closer and closer with each passing second.

4
Ring

"Wow!" exclaimed Will. "Look at the size of that thing! It must be hundreds of miles long!"

In the time it took Will to say that, Major West had navigated a course a safe distance away from the shimmering energy field.

"The energy field is larger than it looks, Will Robinson," said the Robot. "I have computed that the field is an enclosed circle with a radius of one-point-seven-million miles."

"It's a giant-sized light ring!" exclaimed Penny.

"That's incredible!" said Will, astonished. "You could fit a couple of planets and a few stars inside that thing!"

"My sensors are unable to penetrate the energy ring," said the Robot. "However, they do indicate that the ring is not a natural phenomenon."

"You mean somebody made that thing?" asked Penny.

"It contains several synthetic chemical elements," explained the Robot.

"Well, if there is anybody on the other side of it, they obviously want to keep strangers out," said Professor Robinson.

"Yeah," agreed Major West. "Sort of like a high energy 'no trespassing' sign."

"Looks like we'll just have to go around it if we want to reach Will's constellation," said Professor Robinson.

"A journey around the energy ring, even at the *Jupiter 2*'s maximum speed, would take several months," said the Robot.

"Months?" asked Dr. Smith. "You mean we'd have to wait months to go home?"

"If we *can* wait, Dr. Smith," said Professor Robinson. "We've managed to survive in space this long by a combination of hyperdrive leaps and stopovers on environmentally friendly planets where we can regenerate our fuel supply. It's a question of how long we can stay aloft in this area before we need to find someplace to land and refuel."

"Why not just take a hyperdrive leap to that constellation?" asked Dr. Smith.

"Same difference," explained the Professor. "We just took a leap, and an emergency one at that. Right now it could take several weeks just to regenerate the *Jupiter 2*'s hyperdrive core material."

"This is all pseudoscientific drivel!" said Dr. Smith angrily. "The quickest way between two points is straight. I say we blast our way right through that energy ring and head to that constellation before we run out of options."

"But, Dr. Smith, we're not even certain that constellation will lead us home," said Mrs. Robinson.

"Maureen is right," said Professor Robinson. "We'll begin a path around the ring until we can confirm if Will's constellation will lead us home. In the meantime, I don't know about anybody else, but I'm starving for dinner."

"Me, too!" agreed Will. Mealtimes were his favorite times

aboard the *Jupiter 2*. Most of the day was spent following the rules and regulations his father had established. Professor Robinson ran the ship like a professional Air Force vessel: Everyone had specific duties and specific times to perform them. The only rule that was different was mealtime. Here, Professor and Mrs. Robinson insisted that all members of the crew — including Major West and Dr. Smith — sit together at the galley table and eat at the same time while the Robot manned the helm. It was a time when everyone could relax and talk; a time when they were able to forget that they were lost in space billions of light-years away from home; a time for just being together. And although Will enjoyed the responsibilities of being a real spaceman, he sometimes enjoyed just being a ten-year-old kid as well.

"Oh, boy, veggie burgers!" he exclaimed as his parents served dinner a short time later, a job they always did together.

"Penny, you've really tended the solarium soybean crop well," Mrs. Robinson complimented her daughter. "The protein content in these burgers is higher than usual."

"Thanks, Mom," said Penny as she poured some ketchup over her burger.

"Yeah," said Will. "But it takes a lot of this ketchup to make it taste like a *real* burger!"

"That just goes to show you how important it is to grow tomatoes, Will," said Penny. "But if you had your way you'd spend all your time with your nose buried in your computer instead of helping in the solarium."

"It's a good thing, too," Will shot back. "Because now we may have found our way home! Besides, what do you know about star-charting —"

Professor Robinson cleared his throat — loudly. "No arguments at the dinner table, please," he said. Will and Penny quickly stopped arguing and took a bite out of their burgers.

"Don," asked Judy. "Do you really think Will's constellation could be Taurus the Bull?"

"Ninety-three percent does give us the advantage," replied Major West. "But the Robot was right: there's still a seven percent chance against it. In space, those are big odds."

A look of disappointment came over Judy's face. When Major West saw this he gently took her hand in his. "Hey, you know," he told her softly. "Anything's possible."

At that, Will couldn't help himself. He burst out with uncontrollably giddy laughter.

"Penny," he said in a mocking tone. "Anything's possible, you know. And dreams really do come true."

"All right, Will, that's enough," said Major West, blushing. "Hey, where's Smith?" he added suddenly, noticing an empty chair at the table.

"He's usually not late for dinner," said Mrs. Robinson. She went over to the galley intercom and pressed it on. "Dr. Smith," she called into the intercom. "Dinner has been served."

There was no answer.

"Something must be up," said Penny. "Dr. Smith never misses a meal."

"I'll go look for him," said Will. He had just risen from his seat when, without warning, the ship made a sudden jolt that threw him to the floor.

"What was that, John?" asked Mrs. Robinson.

"I don't know. Let's go check it out."

Dinner would have to wait. The entire crew followed Major West upstairs to the control deck.

Once there, they saw that the Robot had been deactivated. And Dr. Smith was sitting behind the main controls navigating the ship directly into the energy ring!

5
Invaders

"Smith!" exclaimed Professor Robinson. He grabbed Smith by the shoulders and pulled him away from the controls. "What do you think you're doing?"

"I was only trying to determine how far we were from the constellation when I accidentally lost control of the ship," explained Dr. Smith sheepishly.

"Accidentally, my eye," said Major West as he took over the controls. Through the viewport everyone could see the energy belt was getting closer. "You set the ship to go right through the energy ring despite Professor Robinson's orders."

Will found the Robot's power pack near the control board.

"Dr. Smith deactivated the Robot!" he said as he reattached the power pack to the metal hull of his mechanical friend.

"I was only trying to help," insisted Smith, not very convincingly.

"I should have jettisoned you in the space pod when I said I would," said Major West.

The ship jolted again as it moved closer and closer toward the shimmering energy mass outside.

"Don, pull us away from here!" ordered Professor Robinson.

"I can't!" replied Major West as he desperately worked the ship's controls. "The centrifugal energy from that ring is too strong! Hold on, everybody. We're going through!"

Just then, the *Jupiter 2* jolted again as the pull of the energy belt took hold of it. Soon the ship was shaking violently. Within seconds, the viewport had become filled with the bright band of light from outside. Seconds after that, the light passed right through the ship's walls engulfing everything — and everyone — inside.

"Activate stabilizers!" ordered Professor Robinson. He, like everyone else, had grabbed onto something as the *Jupiter 2* vibrated wildly.

"Activating stabilizers!" shouted Major West, working the controls as the ship passed through the energy belt. But nothing the handsome young pilot did helped to keep the ship from shaking. "It's not doing any good!"

"Outer hull buckling under pressure from energy belt!" alerted the Robot, now fully reenergized. "T-minus fifty-three seconds before hull breach!"

"Change to vertical course," Professor Robinson ordered Major West. "Pull us out, Don!"

"I can't!" replied Major West as he desperately worked the controls. "Nothing's working!"

"T-minus thirty-three seconds to hull breach!" announced the Robot.

"Somebody do something!" Dr. Smith shouted fearfully.

"Well, if we can't pull out we might as well *push in*," said Major West. "Everybody hold on to your hats!"

Major West reset the controls. The *Jupiter 2*'s engines increased with power and the great ship lunged forward, deeper into the energy ring.

"How long before we pass through the ring?" asked Penny, nervously clutching her mother's hand.

"We're coming out of it now," replied Major West. In seconds the last strands of shimmering energy could be seen fading away.

"Wow," said Will. "That was a close one."

"Is everyone all right?" asked Professor Robinson.

Everyone nodded.

"I'm running an analysis on that energy ring," said Mrs. Robinson, who had already begun reading data from her computer at the life sciences station. She let out a deep sigh of relief. "The ring's electromagnetic properties are non-nucleonic," she said. "It isn't harmful to human life."

"That's a relief," said Judy. "But, just to be on the safe side I want to run a complete physical on each one of us in sickbay. Will and Penny, let's start with you two."

"Sure," agreed Will and Penny together. They followed their sister toward the turbolift just in time to see it rising from below deck.

"Blawp!" exclaimed Penny as Blawp climbed out of the lift. The big-eared, big-eyed leathery-skinned creature strutted happily across deck. Then it jumped into Penny's arms. "It looks like Blawp's okay, too, Dad!"

But no sooner had Penny said that than Blawp suddenly jumped out of her arms. Then she ran into a corner and cowered with fear.

"What made her do that?" Penny wondered aloud. "She practically tore my arm off."

"I wouldn't worry about it, Penny," said Judy reassuringly. "She's probably just a little frightened by all the excitement."

"Negative, Judy Robinson," said the Robot. "Blawp is reacting to its animal instincts. It has detected the presence of an alien."

"You mean an alien spaceship, Robot?" asked Will.

"Negative, Will Robinson," replied the Robot. "This alien needs no spaceship. Look!"

Everyone looked through the viewport. The Robot was right. Outside the spaceship appeared a huge, ugly alien head that must have been as large as the *Jupiter 2* itself. The head seemed to be made of layers of different kinds of skin: part scaly, part smooth, part veins, part ooze. Its two eyes dangled out of their sockets from two mucous-covered ligaments and its mouth held a collection of broken, rotted teeth. It was floating in space all on its own.

Penny grabbed her father's arm in fear. Mrs. Robinson protectively put her arms around her two youngest children and pulled them close. Will tried to keep from trembling. But he couldn't. He had never encountered such a hideous creature before.

Suddenly the alien's loud, deep voice came over the ship's speakers. It spoke in a language no one could understand.

"I'm running that voice through the universal translator," said Mrs. Robinson, moving away from Penny and Will to enter some commands into the computer at her life sciences station. "Let's hope we can get a translation."

Gradually, the alien's language began to change as it became filtered through the translator. Some of its words began to sound like English.

"Alien invaders," it said in an angry tone of voice. "I am the Protector. You have breached the Ring of Joh'el and entered into space that is forbidden to outsiders. This is considered an act of war. For this you will be destroyed!"

6
Protector

Professor Robinson quickly opened a communications link to the alien.

"This is Professor John Robinson of the *Jupiter 2* spaceship," he told the alien. "We are not invaders. We are travelers lost in space. We accidentally passed through your energy shield in an attempt to return home. We mean you no harm. I repeat: We mean you no harm."

Just then, a beam of light shot out from the alien's eyes and passed through the viewport. Then it passed through the rest of the ship and infiltrated all the equipment on board.

"The alien's reading every bit of computer data on board ship!" Will noticed as computer information appeared on all the ship's monitors at an alarming speed.

Seconds later the light receded back into the alien's head.

"I have scanned your history from your vessel's computer libraries," said the alien. "By its evidence you are a warlike lifeform that achieves power by conquering and enslaving others of your species. Now you wish to conquer this space. I cannot permit that."

"It's true," admitted Professor Robinson. "Many humans

have done that. But that's in the far distant past. Today our goals are peaceful."

"Your very existence in space proves you to be a liar, John Robinson," responded the alien. "According to your ship's library your mission was to find a new world to populate because your race had polluted and destroyed your own planet."

"My dad is not a liar!" Will shot back at the alien, no longer frightened. "What he's saying is true. You should at least give us the chance to prove it!"

"Interesting," said the alien, after a pause. "You travel with young offspring on your war vessel."

"We're not a war vessel!" said Penny. "If you scanned our ship's library you should know that."

"Many have tried to invade the Ring of Joh'el," replied the alien. "And many have tried to confuse me with their lies. However, I will consider what your young ones have said. Until then I will place a paralysis field around your vessel so that you may not come any deeper inside the ring. When next I return, it will be with word of your fate."

And with that the monstrous alien disappeared.

For a long moment everyone remained silent, stunned by the alien's threat.

"Dad," said Penny, frightened. "What are we going to do?"

Everyone waited for an answer, but for the first time since they had been in space, it seemed as if Professor Robinson could not come up with one.

"I'm not sure, Penny," said Professor Robinson with a tinge of helplessness in his voice. "I'm not sure."

The next few hours passed slowly. The paralysis field the Joh'ellian Protector had placed around the *Jupiter 2* not only kept it from being able to fly away, it froze practically every instrument on board ship as well.

Professor Robinson and Major West worked tirelessly, trying to find a way to counteract the effects of the paralysis field. But without the use of many of the ship's instruments they had little luck.

There was only one way out, but it was a dangerous one.

"We're going to attempt another hyperdrive leap," Professor Robinson told everybody as soon as he had gathered them together.

"How can we go into hyperdrive while we're surrounded by the paralysis field?" asked Will.

"Chances are the alien will have to release us from the paralysis field if he decides to attack us," explained Will's dad. "Don and I are hoping we can initiate a leap as soon as the field is removed."

"But I thought you said there wasn't enough core material for another hyperdrive leap," Dr. Smith said, remembering.

"There isn't," explained Major West. "But there is enough nucleonic fuel left. John has a theory . . ."

"It's only a theory," added Professor Robinson. "One I've been working on since we've been in space. You see, I've been trying to come up with a way to preserve our fuel supplies by combining them. If I patch our nucleonic fuel distributor to the hyperdrive ion coil we might be able to generate enough power to initiate a small leap."

"Is that enough power to take us away from here?" asked Mrs. Robinson.

"Oh, it'll take us far away from here," said Professor Robinson with certainty. "But, our nucleonic fuel is made of positive-charged electrons while the hyperdrive is based on the harnessing of negative-charged electrons. If my theory works we could end up with another problem . . ."

"I think I know what it is," interjected Will. "There's a possibility the combination of both forms of energy will cancel each other out."

"That's right, Will," said Professor Robinson. "We could be stranded somewhere in space with no fuel supply at all. And if we're not near a planet —"

"We'll just drift forever," groaned Dr. Smith. "Until we die!"

7
Vanished!

Professor Robinson ordered everyone to keep busy with their normal ship's duties while they waited for the Protector to return. That way everyone would be able to keep their minds off the danger they were in. Remembering the condition of the solarium as a result of the electrical storm, Will and Penny returned to clean it up.

Although she busily picked up much of the debris that had fallen during the storm, it was obvious that Penny was worried. Will was worried as well. But as he began helping her clean up, he promised himself not to show it.

"Looks like we'll have to replant these tomato plants," he said as he swept up some plant debris. "We'll need lots of ketchup if you're going to keep making those soy burgers."

Suddenly, Penny stopped what she was doing. She walked close to the solarium window and looked out into the Joh'ellian space.

Will could hear her sobbing quietly. He could tell his sister was unnerved — and his attempt at small talk hadn't helped. He put down the pile of fallen tomato plants he had been sweeping up and joined Penny at the window. He wasn't sure what to do or say.

"I didn't mean it, Penny," said Will, apologetically. "I thought your soy burgers were pretty good. Really, I did."

But Penny didn't seem to be interested in talking about soy burgers.

"It's such an empty space," she said as she stared solemnly outside. "I expected to see more stars and planets inside this ring."

"You heard the Robot say how big the ring is," said Will. "We're probably a half million miles from the nearest Joh'ellian planet."

"They must be a very frightened race of people if they have to shut themselves off from the rest of the universe with that ring," concluded Penny. "They think that we're trying to conquer them in our little spaceship. It's ridiculous!"

"We'll be all right, Penny," said Will bravely.

"You think so, Will?" replied his sister. "I don't think I've ever been so scared in my life."

"Dad's theory makes pretty good sense," Will said, trying to be reassuring. "Interplanetary space cruisers have been combining fuel compounds for years without any problems. I'm sure we'll get out of this okay."

Penny reached out and took Will's hand and gave him a tiny smile. Will smiled back, thinking at first that he had certainly reassured her. But somehow, as he felt his sister's hand tightly squeeze around his, he could tell she knew that he was frightened as well.

Then, without warning, the ship's alarms blasted. Will and Penny suddenly saw a patch of space outside quiver with energy.

"It's the alien!" shouted Will. "He's coming back!"

He and Penny hurriedly ran to the turbolift and joined the others on the control deck. By the time they had arrived, the Protector had returned.

"Humans," said the ugly alien. "Your punishment has been decided. Prepare yourselves."

"Get ready, Don . . ." Professor Robinson whispered to Major West. Major West placed his hand firmly on the hyper-drive initiation control.

Professor Robinson once again opened a communications link to the alien.

"Protector," said Professor Robinson, "I told you we mean you no harm. If you release us we'll leave your space and never return."

"Your punishment has been decided," said the Protector. "No argument you make can change the course of your fate. It has been decided that you, Professor Robinson, and the other elders of your party shall be imprisoned for eternity."

"Imprisoned?" exclaimed Dr. Smith. "This is madness! Why, right now ships from Earth are probably out searching for us. When they find out what you've done to us they'll attack you with unimaginable power!"

"A belligerent statement typical of your hostile race," responded the Protector. "It also serves to prove how dangerous you really are."

"Wait a minute," said Mrs. Robinson, stepping forward. "What did you mean when you said the elders of our party were to be taken prisoner? What about the children?"

"A review of your history has shown me no evidence of children ever willingly participating in any war on your world," said the Protector. "It is obvious that hatred and aggression are taught to them by the adults. Therefore, the Joh'ellians do not hold Will and Penny Robinson responsible for the actions of their parents. They will be free to go in the spaceship with your Robot as their pilot."

"No!" cried Penny.

"We won't do it!" Will shouted as he moved to his parents' side. "We're not going anywhere without our parents!"

"Ah, the sweetness of children," said the Protector. "Even now you see their innocence displayed as I have described. They are better off alone. Prepare yourselves for transfer."

At that, the Protector vanished. Then everyone felt the ship shake with a jolt.

"The paralysis field," said Major West as the *Jupiter 2*'s equipment hummed to life again. "It's been removed!"

"Hyperdrive now, Don!" shouted Professor Robinson.

Major West quickly input the hyperdrive sequence commands into the computer. "Here we go!" he shouted.

But nothing happened. Seconds later, the spaceship was exactly where it had been all along.

"Foolish humans," the Protector's voice echoed over the ship's loudspeakers. "Your plans did not go undetected while your ship was frozen. Your fuel injection system has been neutralized. There is no escape for you. Sentencing will begin."

It happened fast, practically in the blink of an eye. One by one, the adults disappeared. Professor Robinson was the first. He simply vanished before everybody's eyes.

"Dad!" cried Will and Penny as soon as their father disappeared.

Mrs. Robinson and Judy were next, followed by Major West. And even though Dr. Smith had already made a desperate dash for the space pod hatch, he was plucked from the spaceship before he had a chance to escape.

By the time it was all over Will and Penny were the only humans left aboard the *Jupiter 2*.

8
Alone

"They're — *gone*," said Penny, with a shiver. "Mom . . . Dad . . . *everyone!*"

There was an eerie silence on board the *Jupiter 2*. For Will and Penny, the silence seemed almost ghostly.

"We're alone, Penny," said Will. "All alone."

"You are not alone, Will Robinson," said the Robot. "I am here."

"I know, Robot," said Will, unable to break even a small smile. "No offense, but it's not the same."

"I am not programmed to take offense, Will Robinson," replied the Robot, matter-of-factly. Then, in a more understanding tone, the Robot added, "However, I understand how you feel."

Just then, a frightened cry was heard from across the room. It was Blawp.

"Blawp is scared," said Penny as she took Blawp in her arms. "And so am I. I don't want to be alone, Will."

"Neither do I," said Will, with tight, angry lips. "And we're not going to be for long. Not if I can help it."

"What do you mean?" asked Penny.

"If that alien thinks we're just going to turn around and leave the others behind, he's crazy," explained Will. "We're going after them."

"After them? Where?" asked Penny. "We have no idea where the Protector took them."

"Wherever they are, they're inside this energy ring some-where," said Will. "That much we know. All we have to do is start looking."

"Talk about trying to find a needle in a haystack . . ." said Penny.

"Penny is correct," began the Robot. "By my calculations it would take three billion nine hundred —"

Will interrupted. "Don't quote me statistics now, Robot, un-less you have a better idea."

The Robot lowered its dome-shaped head. "Unhappily, I do not, Will Robinson," it admitted.

"All right, then," said Will. "I say we start right away. Agreed?"

"I'm for that," said Penny.

"One thing, Penny," began Will. "We've survived this long in space because Dad always made us follow strict command pro-tocol. Right?"

"Right," agreed Penny.

"I say we do the same. How about you?"

"Agreed."

"All right," said Will. "I'll be the captain, since I kinda know the most about the design of this ship from hanging out with Major West."

"Okay," said Penny. "What am I?"

"You're my second-in-command as well as communications and weapons officer," said Will. "I know it's a lot, but we're kind of short on crew right now."

"What about me, Will Robinson?" asked the Robot.

"That's obvious, Robot," said Will. "You're science officer."

The Robot raised one of its huge arms and saluted Will. "Aye, aye, sir! Science officer reporting for duty!"

"Where do we start looking, Will?" asked Penny. "I mean — Captain Will?" She was eager to begin the search.

Will turned toward the viewport and shrugged. "Thata-way, I guess," he said, pointing straight ahead. Then he sat behind the computer at the robotics station. "We'll start by launching some probes deep into the ring. They're bound to identify some celestial bodies. Then we can plot a course using the probes as guideposts."

"I'll establish a high focus telescopic visual," said Penny as she entered commands into the ship's video systems. "I'll also sweep the area with a series of electromagnetic radio signals. That might give us some idea of what's out there."

"Good thinking, Penny," said Will. "Robot, we'll need your sensors on high alert. Anything you pick up — no matter how small — could be Dad and the others."

"Affirmative, Will Robinson," replied the Robot. "I will expand the parameters of my neurotronic sensor array to comply with the data we will be receiving from the probes."

Once the assignments were doled out Will, Penny, and the Robot performed their tasks quickly and efficiently.

"Probes launched!" Will announced, after releasing probes in all four directions.

"Neurotronic sensors on high scan!" said the Robot.

"High telescopic visuals coming on-screen!" said Penny as she finished adjusting the picture on a group of monitors that hung over her station. Each monitor showed a different angle of the space outside, although none of the pictures yielded anything but black space.

Time passed slowly as Will, Penny, and the Robot waited for a signal — any signal — to come back from space. But after awhile their initial enthusiasm began to dampen.

"Nothing," sighed Penny, after staring into the blank video images on the monitors for some time. "Nothing at all! We're never going to find them! Never!"

"We can't give up now, Penny," said Will. "We just started. Something's got to happen sooner or later. It's just a matter of time."

"Yeah, but how *much* time?" asked Penny anxiously. "Suppose we don't find them for years?"

"Danger! Danger!" the Robot suddenly exclaimed.

"What is it, Robot?" asked Will. "What's wrong?"

"We are approaching an asteroid!" replied the Robot. "And we are on a collision course."

"What asteroid?" asked Penny. "I don't see anything on the monitors."

Notwithstanding Penny's observation, the Robot was right. Without warning, a giant, craggy, black-and-brown moon-sized planetoid appeared in the viewport as if out of nowhere.

And it was getting close.

9
Asteroid

"It's impossible!" exclaimed Will as he leaped into Major West's navigation seat and looked at the radar screen. The screen was blank. "Robot, why didn't our radars pick it up?"

"Because of insufficient data, I cannot answer that question, Will Robinson," replied the Robot. "My sensors are just as surprised as you are at the appearance of the asteroid."

Suddenly, the ship heaved forward, as if it were being yanked by a giant rope.

"What was that?" asked Penny.

"An electromagnetic force from the asteroid is pulling us in," answered the Robot. "Impact is imminent."

"We're going to crash!" exclaimed Penny.

"I'm going to try to pull us out," said Will. "I'm firing the main thruster jets."

Will pounded his finger on the rocket controls. The ship quivered as the thrusters fired, but the asteroid continued to move closer.

"It's not doing any good, Will," said Penny.

"T-minus one minute and fifty-six seconds to impact," announced the Robot.

Now the ship began to shake more wildly as the asteroid's force pulled it closer.

"T-minus one minute and thirty seconds to impact," the Robot continued to count down.

"There's no way out," shouted Will. Thinking quickly, he tried to imagine what Major West might do in this situation. Then it hit him. A flat crash. It was the only way.

"Penny, strap yourself in," he said. "I'm pushing the ship's stabilizers to the max! I'm going to try to angle us so we crash on the ship's underbelly!"

Suddenly, Penny leaped from her seat. "Blawp!" Will heard her cry out with concern. "I've got to get Blawp secured!"

Penny scooped Blawp up in her arms. Despite the vibrations of the ship she carefully led her to a far wall. There she entered a digital code into a wall panel. Seconds later, a section of the wall opened and a landing seat slid out.

"T-minus one minute to impact!" called out the Robot.

Penny hurriedly strapped Blawp into the landing seat.

"Don't worry," Penny said, gently stroking the creature's head. "Everything's going to be all right." Then she blinked her eyes twice at the little creature. It was her way of signaling to her that it would be safe. Blawp, recognizing the secret signal, blinked back. Then she flashed Penny a small, scared smile. Penny tried to smile back, hoping to hide the shudder that traveled down her spine with the knowledge that they might not survive the crash at all.

"T-minus twenty seconds to impact!" announced the Robot.

"Penny!" said Will as he buckled himself into the navigation chair. "Hurry!"

The ship was shaking violently now, so violently that everything looked like one big blur. Any small, loose objects inched their way over the edges of desks and tables. Penny returned to her station and strapped herself into her chair. She noticed right away how hot the chair had become.

"It's getting so warm," she said. "I can hardly breathe!"

"The friction caused by the pull from the asteroid has increased the interior temperature of the ship," explained the Robot. "It is a transitory condition that will vanish upon impact."

Will trembled at the Robot's words. What difference did the warm temperature make if they didn't *survive* the impact? Outside, the asteroid had filled every inch of the wide viewport. It was only a matter of seconds now.

"T-minus ten seconds to impact," continued the Robot. "Nine seconds . . . eight seconds . . ."

Will kept his hand clutched on the ship's stabilizer stick. It was difficult because the electromagnetic force from the asteroid was so great. Still, he knew it was the only chance he had to reduce the force of impact against the huge space rock.

"Four seconds . . ." continued the Robot. "Three . . . two . . . one . . ."

Will closed his eyes and braced himself for the worst. But instead of feeling the ship hit hard on the surface of the asteroid, he felt nothing. All at once the ship had stopped vibrating. And everything felt calm.

Will opened his eyes. The ship wasn't heading into the hard surface of the asteroid anymore. Instead, it had been pulled into a huge, cavernous hole that appeared, as if out of nowhere, in the side of the asteroid. It was a hole that seemed to reach deep inside the moon-sized planetoid, and it seemed to go on forever.

10
Tunnel

"Robot, what happened?" asked Will, as he guided the ship as straight as he could. It was too dark to see much, so he had to rely on the ship's radar sensors to avoid hitting any unseen structures.

"And where are we?" asked Penny, trying her best to adjust her video monitors. "I can't see a thing."

"We have been pulled inside the asteroid," began the Robot. "And are being drawn deeper by the electromagnetic force that has trapped us."

"Inside it?" asked Will. "Then I wasn't imagining things. I'm throwing on some lights."

Will quickly activated the *Jupiter 2*'s exterior spotlights. At once, their surroundings came into view. They were inside the asteroid, all right. It was as if they were traveling through some kind of huge gopher hole. All around the ship was nothing but dark, slimy rock, lit only by the ship's exterior lights.

"Now I know what a worm feels like," quipped Penny. She could clearly see the asteroid tunnel from all sides. It seemed endless.

"At least we're still in one piece," said Will.

"I have a sensor report," announced the Robot.

"Go ahead, Robot," said Will.

"I am receiving several humanoid life signs," reported the Robot. "And they are growing stronger the deeper we travel through the asteroid tunnel."

"Could Dad and the others be down *here*?" Penny wondered aloud.

"My sensors are unable to identify the individual life signs due to interference from the electromagnetic power that is guiding this ship," answered the Robot.

"What is the source of the power, Robot?" asked Will.

"Insufficient data for analysis, Will Robinson," replied the Robot. "I do not know."

"I'm getting an image of something up ahead, Will," said Penny, adjusting the focus on one of the monitors. "It's about twenty miles away. Some kind of opening."

Will slowed the speed of the *Jupiter 2* and awaited the appearance of the opening Penny had described. In a short time they had reached the end of the long tunnel. There was an opening at the end of the tunnel, but it was covered by slimy, dangling moss that looked like something found on rocks along an ocean shore. The closer the ship got to the opening, the stronger the electromagnetic pull on it. Finally, the ship passed through the opening and into a huge cavern cramped with signs of geological age: rocks, stalactites, and multicolored walls of ore-filled stone the size of mountains.

"This is the biggest cave I've ever seen," remarked Penny as she watched the video monitors.

"I'm regaining control of the ship," said Will as he carefully guided the *Jupiter 2* in and around the structures in the cavern. "Whatever was pulling us in has let go."

"Sensor readings of life signs are growing stronger, Will Robinson," said the Robot.

"Maybe we ought to land the ship and look around, Will," suggested Penny.

"That's a good idea, sis," agreed Will. "There's a clear surface up ahead. Prepare for descent."

Will punched in a series of landing coordinates, then he and Penny adjusted their console seats to landing position.

"Approaching landing site," announced Will.

Soon, the ship began to slow down until it came to a full stop, hovering over the spot Will had chosen for the landing.

"Initiating landing rockets," Will said, pressing in the sequence for the powerful rockets that would guide the ship safely to the ground. Next, he added, "Opening main landing support hatches." He pulled a lever and the ship hummed with mechanical activity. Finally, he announced, "Landing rockets on!"

Will pressed a button and a burst of rumbling power could be felt throughout the ship. He and Penny felt the ship lower itself to the ground. It was like being inside a giant elevator as it descended. There was a soft jolt, then the rumbling of the rockets came to a stop.

They had landed.

"Captain checking ship's personnel," said Will as soon as he turned off the ship's motors. "All systems normal. Everybody A-OK?"

"Communications monitors normal," replied Penny with the proper response. "Roger."

"Sensors show science stations operating at one hundred percent," affirmed the Robot.

Will unbuckled his safety belt and stood up. "Robot, run an environmental analysis of the cave," he ordered.

"Aye-aye, Captain," replied the Robot and obediently began running an analysis, a quick procedure signified by the sounds of mechanical whirs and clicks that emanated from its breastplate.

"The outside environment consists of an aggregate of naturally occurring inorganic solids in mostly crystalline form," reported the Robot. "I am reading high levels of calcium, iron, potassium, sodium, and zinc, mostly in the form of stone, salt, sand, and water."

"There's water out there?" asked Will.

"Yes," replied the Robot. "The presence of water confirms that the environment inside this asteroid contains a breathable oxygen for humans."

"All right, then," said Will. "Let's get out there and start looking for those life signs you picked up."

"I'll get Blawp ready," said Penny as she headed for Blawp's landing seat.

"No, Penny," said Will, watching his sister unbuckle Blawp. "I don't think she should come with us."

"Why not?" asked Penny. "I don't want her to be all alone while we're away."

Will hesitated for a moment. He knew how much Blawp meant to his sister, but his gut feeling told him she would just be in the way.

"We don't know what's out there, Penny," explained Will. "I think she'll be safer on board the ship."

"But —" started Penny.

"I'm sorry, Penny," said Will uncomfortably. "That's an order. We agreed, remember?"

Penny nodded. "You're right, Captain." She obviously knew the importance of following orders. She gently kissed Blawp good-bye, and immediately went over to the weapons locker.

"Emergency voiceprint identification number Jupiter-crew-number-six," Penny said into a speaker beside the weapons bay. Both she and Will had been given a special number that they were instructed to use in the event of an emergency only. "Name: Penny Robinson, acting weapons officer."

"Voiceprint confirmed," replied a computerized voice from the speaker. Then the windows on the weapons bay slid open. Penny pulled out two rifles and threw one of them to Will.

"Make sure you deactivate the safety on that thing," Penny reminded her brother.

"Roger," said Will. He made sure the laser rifle was in working order, then flung it across his back when he was done.

Next, Will pulled two utility belts from a nearby closet. Each belt was fully equipped with rope and tackle, digital chemical analyzers, and all-purpose laser knives. He gave one belt to Penny and strapped the other around his waist. Finally, he gave a small communicator to his sister and kept one for himself. Then he opened the main air lock. A surge of cool, damp air rushed in from the cavern.

"Ready?" Will asked his sister.

"Ready when you are."

Will nodded and let out an apprehensive sigh. Without any further ado he cautiously led Penny and the Robot out of the spaceship. Within minutes, they had climbed down the landing supports and stepped onto the floor of the cavern. Although the floor looked as if it were made of solid rock, Will and Penny could feel their feet sink slightly into the ground.

"The ground is soft," said Penny. "It feels kind of like a — a cushion of some kind."

"The ground is covered by a thin gelatinous membrane," said the Robot. "For some reason my sensors are unable to configure its function. However, I will continue to run an analysis as more data comes in."

"Robot," started Will. "How far away are those life signs you were reading?"

"The first reading is coming from three-point-nine kilometers in that direction," said the Robot, pointing deeper into the cavern. Will could see only as far as the *Jupiter 2*'s great spotlight could illuminate. Beyond that was only darkness.

"Then let's start walking," he said.

It took only a short while to reach the edge of the darkness. Once there, Will and Penny turned on their high-beam laser rifle lights and aimed them ahead.

"The life signs are becoming stronger," said the Robot. "We are almost upon their source."

Penny tried to see into the darkness, but the beam from her rifle light revealed only more of the cavern.

"Penny," said Will, stopping. "Did you hear something?"

Penny stopped and listened. "No," she said.

"Listen," said Will. "That *sound . . .*"

Will, Penny, and the Robot became very still as they listened, but all that could be heard was the whoosh of a slight wind.

"It's just wind," said Penny.

"No," said Will. "It sounds like a whisper."

"Will . . . Penny . . . help us . . ." came the faint sound of a voice.

"Someone's *calling* us!" said Penny.

"Not just someone," said Will. "It sounds like — !"

Before he could finish his sentence three ghostly figures appeared a few feet ahead of them.

"Mom, Dad, Judy!" exclaimed Will.

"Will, Penny . . ." said Mrs. Robinson. *"Help us, help us, please . . ."*

44

Will and Penny's parents and sister were reaching out to them. Their eyes were pleading, searching. Their bodies were semitransparent, floating in space. Will and Penny could see right through them.

"Mom!" Penny ran toward the image of her mother. But by the time she had taken a few steps, her mother, father, and sister vanished into thin air.

"They're gone!" said Will. "Robot, did you see them?"

"Affirmative, Will Robinson," replied the Robot. "However, my sensors indicate that they were there, yet they were *not* there!"

"What do you mean, Robot?" asked Will.

"Your parents are trapped between a bend in time and space that is opening and closing at random," replied the Robot. "Somehow we were able to witness them for a brief moment."

"Was it some kind of projection, Robot?" asked Penny.

"Negative, Penny Robinson," replied the Robot. "When your parents appeared their life readings became stronger. Now they are distant again."

"Mom? Dad? Judy?" she called out. "If you're out there can you hear us? It's Penny."

Will, Penny, and the Robot waited for an answer, but none came. After a few moments they stepped into the dark area. They had barely taken a step when they froze with terror, their light beams revealing a horrifying sight. Strewn all over the cavern were skeletons, hundreds of them. They were of all different shapes and sizes, and none of them looked human.

Then, from out of the darkness ahead, came the loudest, most blood-curdling scream any of them had ever heard.

11
Predator

"What in the known universe was that?" shrieked Penny, with a jump.

"I don't know," said Will, as soon as he stopped trembling. "But it came from farther down."

Without warning the scream came again. Will and Penny swirled around. This time it seemed closer.

When the scream came a third time, it was accompanied by a loud flapping sound, like a sail being blown in the wind. A strong breeze brushed along the floor of the cavern and Will and Penny had the sensation that something had just flown by them.

"Danger!" said the Robot. "An alien presence is close by!"

"What kind of alien, Robot?" asked Will. "Is it the Protector?"

"Negative, Will Robinson," said the Robot. "But my sensors tell me its intentions are hostile."

Will and Penny swallowed with fear. They aimed their rifles into the darkness, crisscrossing their light beams as they did so.

"Over there!" shouted Penny. Her light beam settled on a ledge high in the cavern wall. For a split second something could be seen: a hunched figure so black it looked at first like a shadow. Large and lean, the shadowy figure darted out of the rifle's light beam.

"Ready rifles," said Will, nervously cocking his rifle's laser settings. Penny did the same. The Robot extended its arms and aimed its pointed laser pincers straight ahead. When everyone was ready, Will gave the order to advance.

They moved slowly and carefully, trying to keep their balance on the soft mucouslike floor of the cavern, and keeping a lookout for the dark creature they knew lurked somewhere in the shadows ahead.

Once again they heard the flapping sound. Once again a gust of wind passed over them.

"Danger! Danger!" alerted the Robot. "The predator is near!"

"Over there!" said Will, swerving around. Thinking he spotted the predator, he let out a blast from his rifle. But he was wrong. Instead of hitting the mysterious predator, the laser beam exploded into a harmless pile of rocks.

"Look out, Will!" shouted Penny. "Behind you!"

Will started to turn, but it was too late. The dread figure of the shadowy predator swooped down from a crevice above. For an instant, Penny could see the creature clearly in the beam from her rifle light. It was a huge thing with two batlike wings that spread several feet across and carried it almost gracefully through the air. Its body was lean and muscular and covered with a short, gray fur. It had two long arms and legs, and was almost human-looking, but its face was like that of a mouse, with two black eyes.

It was some kind of giant bat-creature. And in an instant it had swooped down and plucked Will from the ground, engulfing him in its strong, lean arms. Taken by surprise, Will dropped his laser rifle. Then he was carried by the bat-creature into one of the many crevices high in the cavern's ceiling.

"Will!" he could hear Penny cry out as he felt himself being carried away by the creature.

Penny's cries soon grew dim and the walls around him swirled as Will felt himself being lifted higher and higher. The bat-creature hovered near a small hole high in the cavern wall. Finally, it carried Will inside the hole and set him down inside a cave. It was dark inside the cave — so dark that Will could hardly see anything around him. In a few seconds, however, his eyes adjusted to the gloom. That's when he noticed that the cave was filled with more piles of skeletal remains. That's when he also realized the bat-creature was moving toward him, its ratlike mouth open to reveal a set of glistening, hungry-looking fangs.

12
Lair

"Will!" Penny's voice crackled over his communicator. "Are you all right?"

The bat-creature suddenly stopped moving toward Will. For no apparent reason, it suddenly turned around and flew out of the cave. When he was sure the creature was a safe distance away, Will raised his communicator to his lips.

"Will, can you hear me?" came Penny's voice again. "Will, do you read me? Are you all right?"

"I read you, Penny," replied Will. "I'm okay for now. The bat-creature flew away, but I have a feeling he'll be back. I'm in some kind of small cave. And I'm surrounded by skeletons."

"Can you escape?" asked Penny.

"I'm not sure," replied Will. He carefully stepped over to the mouth of the cave and peered out. He could see Penny and the Robot on the floor of the cave, hundreds of feet below. "I'm pretty high up."

"You are exactly one thousand three hundred sixty-six yards from the ground of the cavern, Will Robinson," said the Robot. "And although my sensors indicate there are several

49

ways to reach the upper levels of the cavern, most of them would take too long."

"Too long?" asked Penny. "What do you mean?"

"Judging by the skeletal remains we have found here I have computed that the bat-creature is a carnivore," explained the Robot.

"You mean it's a meat-eater?"

"Yes," replied the Robot. "I have also computed that it is hungry and desires a warm-blooded lunch."

"You mean — Will —?" Will could hear Penny shudder when she spoke. It didn't take a wild stretch of the imagination to figure out why.

"Yes, Penny Robinson," said the Robot. "It is my conclusion that the bat-creature intends to make lunch out of your brother."

"Will, you've got to get out of there!" urged Penny. She directed her light beam along the wall below the small cave that now held Will. "I can see a ledge below the cave."

"I see it, too, Penny," replied Will. "I'm going to have to try to reach it using my rope and tackle."

Will waved an okay signal to Penny and the Robot. Then he tossed out his rope until it dangled down the side of the wall. It fell just several feet short of the ledge.

"My rope's not long enough," said Will. "I'm going to try to climb down as far as I can, and then jump the rest of the way."

"Be careful, Will," said Penny. "If you miss, you could be killed!"

But by then Will had dug the spikes of his tackle between some rocks at the mouth of the bat-creature's lair. He threw the rest of the rope over the side. He yanked at the rope to make sure it was taut. Once he was satisfied that the rope could support him, he carefully began climbing down the wall of the cavern. He moved slowly, holding tightly to the rope with the strength of his back and making sure one foot was firmly planted on the cavern wall before moving the other.

When he reached the end of the rope he dangled, his feet hovering the few feet away from the ledge. He was just about to leap the rest of the way when a huge shadow fell across him.

It was the bat-creature. It swooped down on Will, plucked him off of the rope, carried him back up, and deposited him into the darkness of its lair.

Will cowered against a wall as the bat-creature stepped toward him. The creature now had something in its hands. It was a gooey, stringlike substance that looked as if it had been scraped off the walls of the cavern. It reached forward and Will knew that the bat-creature was going to wrap the substance around him, probably to prevent him from trying to escape again.

Without taking his eyes off the mousy-looking bat's face, Will reached behind him for his laser knife. But no sooner had he turned it on and raised it in defense than the bat-creature swiped it out of his hand. Will cowered helplessly against the wall. He reached down, groping for anything that might help him fight off the creature. Feeling something hard he picked it up. It was a bone with fresh, half-chewed flesh still hanging off its edges. He brought the bone down against the bat-creature, but only managed to knick the thing's shoulder before it swiped that, too, out of Will's hands.

Will knew that there was nothing else he could do. As the bat-creature began to tie him up, Will opened his mouth to scream.

13
Quake

Will was so frightened that no sound came out of his mouth. He lay there soundlessly as the bat-creature shrouded him in the gooey substance until the only thing Will was able to move was his head. Will was trapped like a fly in a spider's web. And like a fly, Will knew, it was only a matter of time before he would be eaten alive. His only hope was Penny and the Robot. But they were so far away, at the base of the cavern, he felt certain they could never reach him in time.

Then he heard something from outside the cave. It was a mechanical sound, like that of a motor being revved up. Soon the sound began to grow louder, as if it were rising up from below.

The bat-creature must have heard the sound as well, reasoned Will, because it turned away and headed to the mouth of its lair to see what the strange sound was.

All at once, a bright, blinding light appeared in the mouth of the cave. The light was so bright, at first Will thought it was some kind of tiny sun. Whatever it was, Will had to squint his eyes.

The bat-creature, however, had a more violent reaction. It began to shriek with fear. It raised its huge bat-wings and covered its eyes. It swerved around and ran deeper into the cave, trying desperately to find a dark spot in which to hide, but there was none. The cave was completely lit up and now everything inside could be seen in all its hideousness. Against the farthest end of the cave, the bat-creature cowered, wrapped in its wings for protection from the encroaching light.

"Will, can you hear me?" came a voice from outside the cave. It was Penny.

"Penny —?" asked Will.

"Thank goodness we're in time," said Penny with a sigh of relief. "We're coming in."

The light now moved directly into the cave. In a matter of seconds, Will saw Penny and the Robot. Both were wearing jet packs, the source of the mechanical sound, and were hovering at the mouth of the cave. Together they held one of the *Jupiter 2*'s huge arc lamps, the portable kind that was normally used for lighting fuel-drill sites on alien planets. The arc lamp's internal liquid crystal power source was so powerful it could make night seem like day.

Penny and the Robot quickly lowered themselves into the cave, turning their jet packs off as they did. Then they set the arc lamp in a position so that the entire cave remained bright.

"Am I glad to see you two!" said Will with a smile.

Penny raced over to her brother. She pulled her laser knife out and swiftly began burning away at the cocoon that shrouded Will.

"It was my idea to use the jet packs to get up here quickly," explained Penny. "But it was the Robot who figured out how to scare the bat-creature."

"How was that, Robot?" asked Will.

"I observed that the bat-creature never made an appearance in the light," explained the Robot. "This was not unlike the natural instinct of bats on Earth, who prefer the darkness of caves and rarely expose themselves to daylight. I concluded a sudden bright blast of light might startle the bat-creature enough to give us time to rescue you."

"Good thinking, Robot," said Will as he felt his body become free of his slimy bonds.

"Correction, Will Robinson," said the Robot. "Robots do not think. My conclusion was based on a logical neurosensor computation."

Will walked over to the Robot. "Good computing, then," he said, patting the Robot on the back.

"And now," began the Robot. "To make certain of your future safety while we are inside this asteroid, I will destroy the bat-creature."

"No, Robot," said Will. He could see the bat-creature hovering against the wall, its back to them, shaking with fear. "It was just trying to survive by its natural instincts. It was really *us* who invaded *his* world. Besides, the liquid crystals of the arc lamp will burn for days. We'll be long gone by then."

"If those are your orders, I will obey," said the Robot. "You are safe and well and I am glad of that."

"Shouldn't we be getting out of here?" asked Penny.

Will agreed. He climbed onto the Robot's back. Within minutes Penny and the Robot restarted their jet packs and the three of them landed back on the cavern floor.

"Let's put the jet packs away and continue on through the tunnel," said Will, climbing down from the Robot's back.

It was just as they started back toward the *Jupiter 2* that they heard, *"Will! Penny! Help us ..."*

Two men were calling from directly ahead of them.

"It's Major West —!" said Penny.

"And Dr. Smith!" added Will.

Major West and Dr. Smith were standing in front of the *Jupiter 2*. Just like the earlier figures of the children's family, the two men were only faintly visible.

"Robot, are they really here?" asked Will.

"They are very close," replied the Robot, "but they are also very far."

"Major West! Dr. Smith!" called Penny. "Can you hear us?"

"We can hear you," said Major West. "Can you get a fix on our location?"

"The Robot tells us that you're in between some kind of bend in time and space," explained Will. "If we could get back to the ship in enough time to take a reading —"

Suddenly, the children felt a jolt as the ground began to shake beneath them.

"What's happening, Robot?" asked Penny as she struggled to keep her balance.

"My sensors are measuring a massive seismic movement caused by the release of stress accumulated along several of the asteroid's nearby geologic faults," answered Robot.

"You mean an earthquake!" exclaimed Will.

The tremors grew with intensity. Will was thrown to the ground.

"Will!" cried out Penny.

Will saw his sister making her way toward him when, without warning, there was a thunderous blast. The ground beneath Penny's feet cracked open like a fragile eggshell. She was suddenly sucked down into a deep, dark abyss, followed by a stream of dirt and tiny stones. And there was nothing Will could do but stand and watch.

14
Lava

Will raced to the newly formed hole in the ground and peered into it. He could see nothing but darkness.

"Penny!" Will cried out. "Penny, can you hear me?"

There was no answer.

"Robot, we've got to get down there — fast!" Will said.

"Affirmative, Will Robinson," replied the Robot. "But what about Major West and Dr. Smith?"

Will looked back toward the ghostly figures. Major West and Dr. Smith were already beginning to vanish.

"Penny is more important right now," said Will.

"Very well," said the Robot. "Climb on. We will descend into the hole and search for your sister."

Once again, Will climbed onto the Robot's back. Then the Robot turned on its jet pack, stepped closer to the hole formed by the earthquake, and jumped in.

The descent seemed to take forever. As Will felt himself being lowered deeper into the belly of the asteroid, he realized that the hole must be several miles deep. He knew that it would have taken nothing less than a miracle for Penny to survive her fall.

"I'm getting hot, Robot," commented Will. The farther they descended the warmer it was becoming.

"My sensors are picking up very high temperatures from the landing below," said the Robot. "I am also picking up readings of high volcanic activity."

In a few seconds, the darkness gave way to a red-and-orange glow that seemed to light the way. Will looked down and saw the source of the glow: a flowing river of molten lava. On either side of the river were steep shores of dark, solid rock. The Robot slowed his descent as they approached the lava bed, then began flying parallel to it.

"I will land on one of the embankments," said the Robot. "Despite the heat generated from the lava bed, the solid rock surrounding it is sufficiently cool for you to walk on."

Once they landed, Will wasted no time. "Do you read Penny's life signs?" he asked the Robot, all the while fearing the worst.

"Negative, Will Robinson," replied the Robot. "Oddly enough, I read nothing at all."

The Robot's answer surprised Will. "What do you mean, Robot?"

"I mean that I cannot tell if your sister is alive or dead," explained the Robot. "Just as I could not tell that we were approaching this asteroid when we were in space. And I have yet to be able to compute a complete analysis of this asteroid's geological makeup. For example, this internal lava bed did not register on my sensors before the earthquake — and it should have."

"I agree, Robot," said Will. "Is something wrong with your sensor array?"

"Negative," replied the Robot. "My systems check out at one hundred percent."

"Then why can't you tell if Penny is alive or not?" demanded Will.

"I cannot explain any further at this time, Will Robinson," said the Robot. "There is too much contradictory data that my computers must analyze. I suggest we begin a search for your sister."

Will was about to agree when he heard a soft moan from somewhere behind him. He pulled his laser rifle from around his back and aimed it in the direction of the sound.

"It's coming from over there," said Will, pointing to some rocks on the embankment.

The moan came again. Will and Robot moved cautiously toward the rocks. Will's eyes widened as he stared fixedly at the rocks, red-hued with the light from the nearby lava bed. Then there was a movement. Will's heart leaped as he readied his fingers on the trigger of his rifle. Something had fallen out from behind the rocks. It wasn't until he got within a few feet of it that he realized what it was.

It was a hand. Penny's hand.

"Penny!" Will cried out as he slung his rifle around his shoulder and ran behind the rocks. Penny lay there, dazed. Her face and hands were cut and bruised. Her jet pack, still strapped to her back, had snapped in two.

"Penny, can you hear me?" Will asked.

"Yes," Penny said, a bit groggily.

Will quickly pulled a canteen of electrolyte-purified water from his utility belt and helped Penny to drink it.

"Take it easy, sis," Will said, reassuringly. "You're going to be all right."

"If it hadn't been for my jet pack," began Penny, "I wouldn't be all right at all. I managed to keep my cool and turn it on just before hitting the ground. Will, where are we?"

"We are approximately six and one-half kilometers closer to the core of this asteroid," said the Robot. "We are also very close to the humanoid life signs we have been trailing."

"Which way, Robot?" asked Will.

The Robot extended its arm and pointed back toward the stone embankment. "That way," it replied.

"Can you walk all right, Penny?" asked Will as he helped his sister to her feet.

"My ankle's a little sore," she answered, testing her balance. "Other than that, I'm all right. What are we going to do now?"

"Follow the Robot's sensor readings and hope they'll lead us to Mom and Dad and the others," said Will. "Lead the way, Robot."

The Robot guided Will and Penny deeper into the asteroid, through low-ceilinged rocky passageways that led away from the river of lava. The orange glow from the steaming lava bed was so strong it lit their path as they went. The farther they walked, the more craggy the rocky landscape became. Soon it was difficult to walk without stumbling.

"Warning! Warning!" the Robot shouted, coming to an abrupt stop. "We are surrounded by aliens!"

"Where, Robot?" asked Will, aiming his laser rifle straight ahead. But there were no signs of aliens. "I don't see anything. Are you sure your sensors aren't going haywire?"

"Negative, Will Robinson," replied the Robot. "We are definitely surrounded!"

The Robot had hardly finished speaking when Will heard a movement from behind. He and Penny spun around at the sound. At first, it looked as if the very rocks that surrounded them were literally bending out of shape. Several of them seemed to actually grow in size.

That's when Will realized that the rocks weren't growing at

all. They were rising up as if from a long, dormant sleep. Some rose up from the ground, others simply poured right out of the walls. And now he could see their shape: They had long, bulky torsos and thick, threatening arms.

Will and Penny stepped back in horror, but there was no place to run. They were surrounded.

15
Shadow

Will, Penny, and the Robot crouched together, trapped inside the circle of rock monsters. With each passing second the rock monsters lumbered inward with steps made with feet the size of small boulders.

Will aimed his laser rifle and fired, hitting one of the rock monsters and smashing it to bits. But no sooner had the smashed rock bits of the creature hit the floor than it began to rise up again — this time as several smaller creatures.

"They're indestructible!" said Will in astonishment.

"Will! Help!" cried Penny. She had taken out her rope and tackle and had tried to lasso one of the rock creatures to the ground. But the creature grabbed the rope and was pulling Penny into its clutches. Penny pulled out her laser knife and tried to break free of the creature's stony grip by slicing into its arms with her weapon, but the short bursts of laser energy were no match for the rock monster.

"Help!" cried Penny again, feeling the rock creature's grip tightening around her waist. "It's crushing me!"

Will and the Robot ran to Penny. Afraid of shooting the craggy alien for fear of hitting Penny, Will took his laser rifle

61

by the nozzle and used it like a club, hitting the creature with repeated blows to its legs. Unfazed by the blows, the monster continued to squeeze Penny.

"Will!" shrieked Penny, a hand flying up to touch her dark hair. "What's happening?"

Will watched in wide-eyed horror as he saw what was left of Penny's hair. Strands of it were being absorbed into the rock creature's head. The more her hair disappeared, the larger the rock creature was becoming.

"The rock alien is absorbing the mineral content of Penny's body," said the Robot. "It is literally gaining nourishment through her. I will attempt to separate them."

The Robot grabbed the rock creature's arms and tried to pry them loose from Penny. It was unsuccessful until it released an electrical charge from its laser-ready claws. This forced the rock creature's grip to loosen. Penny fell to the ground, catching her breath as she landed.

"Are you all right, Penny?" asked Will.

"Yeah," replied Penny, patting her head. "Is my hair back to normal?"

Will couldn't keep from smiling at Penny's concern. "Don't worry," he said. "You look fine."

But the danger wasn't over yet. They were still surrounded by the rock creatures.

"Quickly, get behind me," the Robot told Will and Penny. "If the rock creatures capture you they will completely absorb you for nourishment. I will reconfigure my internal lasers and emit a high photon energy field. That should give you enough time to escape."

"Negative, Robot," responded Will, his heart leaping with fear at what a laser reconfiguration might do to the Robot.

"Your internal systems were not designed to sustain such a high stimulation of energy. If you maintain a force field too long —"

"Affirmative, Will Robinson," interrupted the Robot. "If I maintain a high level of electron stimulation for too long I will be destroyed. But, at the moment, we have no choice. If these aliens can be incapacitated — if just for a short time — you and Penny will be able to escape."

"Robot, I said no," insisted Will. "You're too valuable to us to be destroyed. That's an order."

"It is my main function to ensure *safe and hospitable environmental conditions for the Robinson family*," replied the Robot. It was repeating its original programming directive. "This environment is clearly not a hospitable one — so I will make it one!"

The Robot shoved Will and Penny behind its body. In an instant, its internal mechanisms began to hum with electronic power. In a few short seconds, the hum grew to a high-pitched level. In another few seconds, a powerful light shield appeared around the Robot. The energy from the shield was so strong it kept the rock creatures at bay.

"Run!" the Robot told the children. "Now is your chance. I can keep the creatures away for only another thirty-five seconds and counting . . ."

"Robot, no!" cried Will, not wanting to leave his friend behind. But even as he spoke he could see the Robot's force shield weakening. The rock creatures were beginning to break through.

"Will, we've got to make a run for it," said Penny, pulling her brother by the arm. "The Robot's right. It's our only chance if we want to save the others."

Will knew his sister was right. "We'll be back, Robot," he said as he followed Penny away from the rock creatures. "I promise, we'll be back!"

Will followed his sister deeper into the craggy passageways that lay ahead. They had barely run a few yards when they saw something up ahead that made them stop and cringe. It was a shadow — a huge, monstrous shadow. Something was hiding just beyond the next turn.

16
Doby

Even though his heart was pounding with fear, Will pointed his rifle steadily at the shadow. Penny stood beside him, bravely wielding her laser knife with her shaking hand.

"It's coming closer," said Penny. "Whatever it is."

Even as she spoke the shadow grew in size. At any moment, the children expected to see some giant, hideous-looking menace pop out and attack them. Their eyes widened and stared with horror at the dark shadow.

Soon a large head, about the size of a basketball, came into view. Will and Penny could clearly see a small, three-cornered cap sitting somewhat crookedly on a clot of dark curly hair on top of the head, all of which was offset by a pair of distinctly triangular ears.

Next came the shoulders. But to the children's surprise, the shoulders of this figure were far smaller than they had expected. In fact, they were positively *tiny*, as were its arms and legs, all of which floated behind its oversized head.

The giant monster the children had expected was, in actuality, a miniscule creature less than a foot tall. Its giant shadow was only the result of the unusual lighting in the underground cavern.

"Out of my way!" said the figure as it appeared around the bend and zoomed straight toward Will and Penny.

Will and Penny stepped aside, momentarily stunned by the sight of the pixieish creature, and allowed it to fly by them. The creature flew straight toward the circle of rock creatures that had, by now, engulfed the Robot completely and were beginning to tear it apart.

From a belt around its waist the creature pulled out what looked to Will to be a kind of lasso. Only this lasso wasn't made of rope. It was made of light. Swinging the lasso high above its large head the little flying creature tossed it around one of the rock creatures and pulled it away from the Robot. One squeeze of the lasso by the little flying alien and the rock creature turned into a pile of white dust.

"Run, Mr. Robot!" said the tiny alien as it proceeded to lasso another rock monster and turn it into dust like the first one.

The Robot obeyed the alien and hurried to join Will and Penny. In the meantime, the little creature pulled out a tiny pistol from a holster strapped to its waist and began firing light bolts at the other rock creatures. Each creature turned to dust as soon as it was hit.

"Robot, are you all right?" asked Will with concern.

"Except for a loosened bumper plate I am still fully operational," replied the Robot.

"You can't say the same for those rock creatures," noticed Penny. "They're nothing more than rock dust now."

It was true. The strange little flying alien had lassoed and disintegrated each one of the rock menaces. With one flick of its wrist it returned its glowing lasso to its belt and faced

Penny and Will. Then it twirled its pistol on its finger, returned it to its holster, and floated back to Will and the others.

"I hope y'all are all right." Its accent reminded Will of someone from an old cowboy holograph-movie. It had a Western twang. "Those fellers been reduced to their trace elements. A little technique I picked up while surviving down here in the wild."

"We're okay, thanks to you," said Will.

"Ain't a safe place fer young 'uns like yerselves to be wanderin' about unsupervised," said the little creature. "Do yer folks know where yer at?"

"I'm Penny Robinson," Penny introduced herself. "And this is my brother, Will. We're from Earth. Our parents were kidnapped and we're looking for them."

"I'm pleased to meet y'all," said the flying alien. "I'm a Doby, the last of my kind. You're lookin' at a real relic!"

"Do you live down here?" asked Will.

"I wouldn't exactly call this *livin'*," said the Doby with a chuckle. "No, I've been down here so long I forgot what it's like to talk with other beings. Intelligent ones, anyway."

"You mean, you're trapped inside this asteroid, too?" asked Penny.

"That's exactly it, li'l' lady," replied the Doby. "I was with a wagon train of travelers from my planet. We accidentally passed through that shiny energy ring out there —"

"The Ring of Joh'el!" exclaimed Will. "That's the same thing that happened to us!"

"Before we knew it some huge varmint was threatening us," continued the Doby. "Telling us he was going to destroy us for trespassin'! Now me, I don't take much to threats. Me and the others managed to escape in a small nuclear-powered surrey. But it weren't too long 'fore we got sucked into this rock. Our surrey ran out of fuel, then it got picked apart by that bat-thing that lives upstairs. Then those rock creatures attacked. They ate up my crew. I've been here sparrin' with them ever since."

"You mean there are more of those creatures down here?" asked Will.

"That's one I could never figger out, Willy-boy," said the Doby. "Seems as soon as I disintegrate one bunch of those crit-ters a whole new herd comes out of the walls and the ground. Seems they have some kind of carbon-silicon-based physiol-ogy. This place seems to be some kind of breeding ground for rock monsters."

"Our spaceship!" said Penny with alarm. "If any of those rock creatures find our spaceship we'll be trapped here forever!"

"Spaceship?" asked the Doby. "You have a working space-ship? That means we can get out of here, that is — if you don't mind me taggin' along. I make a mighty mean bowl of cosmic chili, you know."

"We're travelers lost in space," explained Will. "We thought we may have found a course home when we accidentally tres-passed into Joh'ellian space. The Protector kidnapped our par-ents and our Robot thinks they might be inside this asteroid. We can't leave until we find them."

"I hate to be the one to bring bad news, Willy-boy," said the Doby, "but I been down in this asteroid for so long I know every inch of it. I ain't seen any Earth people here."

"The Doby is correct, Will Robinson," added the Robot.

"What do you mean, Robot?" asked Penny.

"I have just rescanned my sensor array," replied the Robot. "I am no longer picking up any humanoid life signs in this asteroid. They have vanished as mysteriously as they ap-peared."

17
Bomb

"You don't pick up any humanoid life signs *at all*?" Penny asked the Robot with surprise. "You mean Dad, Mom, and the others are not even here? But that doesn't make any sense."

"Correction, Penny Robinson," said the Robot. "It is the only thing that *does* make sense."

"Explain, Robot," said Will.

"Ever since we passed through the energy ring nothing that we have encountered has registered with my sensors," said the Robot. "Asteroids appear without warning. Earthquakes and lava beds do not read. Life signs are intangible and time and space bend at random. Normal computer logic seems to have no meaning in Joh'ellian space. There can be only one explanation."

"What's that?" asked Penny.

"This space exists in a different dimension from ours," concluded the Robot. "A dimension in which space and time are not governed by the laws of physics. In other words, you can't trust anything you see."

"If that's so, how are we ever going to find the others?" Will sighed. "They might even be here in this asteroid, only we'd never know it."

"Or they could be anywhere in this freaky dimension," added Penny.

"But with your spaceship," began the Doby. "Y'all can rustle yourselves outta here — maybe even break back through that energy ring and continue on that course home you said you found."

"What would be the point without the rest of our crew?" asked Will.

"Yeah," agreed Penny. "It wouldn't be the same. I vote we stay inside the ring until we find everybody — or die trying. What do you say, Will?"

Will smiled. "Did you have to ask, Penny? As far as I'm concerned 'Operation: Rescue' is still in effect. Sorry, Doby. We'll be happy to take you with us out of the asteroid, but we're not going to leave Joh'ellian space without our family."

"Whoooopeeeee!" shouted the Doby with such excitement he did a somersault in midair. "You humans sure are as spunky as a wild space horse!"

"Then you're with us?" asked Will. "We can sure use an extra hand."

"I'm with yer all the way, Willy-boy! When do we start?"

"I guess we can start right now," said Will. "Let's go back to the spaceship and see if there's some way to get out from inside this asteroid," said Will.

It took only a short time to return to the *Jupiter 2*. The Robot still had a jet pack strapped to its back so Will and Penny simply hitched onto its back as it flew out of the hole made by the earthquake and back to the upper level. The Doby flew along, never touching the ground even after they had landed above. Instead it followed through the air as Will, Penny, and the Robot walked back to their spaceship.

"Hooowheee!" shouted the Doby upon seeing the *Jupiter 2*. "Look at the size of that critter! You can practically fit my whole planet in there!"

"This ship was designed for intergalactic travel," explained Will. "It was supposed to take us to a planet called Alpha Prime before we got knocked off course."

Once inside the *Jupiter 2* Penny was greeted with hugs from Blawp. After a quick examination of the creature, Penny was satisfied that she was safe.

In the meanwhile, Will removed the jet pack from the Robot and returned it to the utilities closet. Afterward he sat at the controls and checked the ship's operating status.

"Everything still seems to be working fine," he said. "How's everything on visual, sis?"

Penny viewed the ship's video monitors. "Video station A-OK," she reported. "I'll start scanning the video playback for the time we were gone."

"Robot, can you calculate a trajectory out of the asteroid?" asked Will.

"In order for us to leave this asteroid we must first locate our point of entry," replied the Robot.

"That shouldn't be too hard," said Will. "We came in through a tunnel located at three-three-seven-mark-nine, according to the ship's flight recorder. We'll leave the same way we came in."

"Check again, Will Robinson," said the Robot. "There is no such tunnel at that location."

"The Robot's right, Will," said Penny. "Our cameras can't find any sign of the tunnel we came through. All I see are solid walls."

"Another anomaly created by this different dimension, Robot?" asked Will.

"That is a logical assumption," replied the Robot.

"Then how do we get out of here?" asked Penny.

"A ship this size must have a mighty strong ability to deflect space debris," said the Doby. "Am I right?"

"The *Jupiter 2* is fully equipped with nuclear-force high energy shields capable of withstanding nearly one million tons of pressure," replied the Robot.

"Well, I'll be!" exclaimed the Doby. "Gettin' outta here's gonna be a cinch."

"You know the way out?" asked Penny.

"I know how to *make* a way out," said the Doby. "When I first got here I tried to blast my way out. But my ship was too small and my force shields too weak. With the *Jupiter 2* we can surround ourselves with a force field that'll protect us."

"Protect us from what?" asked Will.

"From the explosion."

"What explosion?" asked Penny.

"The one that's gonna happen after I place a phase-one photon bomb right out there," replied the Doby, pointing to an area in the cavern outside. "I'm gonna explode this asteroid from the inside out!"

"But nothing can survive that kind of blast!" exclaimed Will. "The *Jupiter 2* will be blown to bits — and us along with it!"

72

18
Continuum

"Don't go turnin' chicken on me now, Willy-boy," said the Doby. "You wanna get outta this here territory, don't you?"

"It's not me I'm concerned about," said Will. "You're right. The *Jupiter 2* may be able to survive a phase-one photon bomb blast with our force shields at full intensity. But there are things out there in that asteroid. *Living* things."

"Living things?" asked the Doby. "What kind of living things?"

"That bat-creature for one," said Penny. "All it wants to do is survive."

"Survive?" laughed the Doby. "That thing would eat you just for blinking at it."

"And those rock creatures," said Will. "I'm glad you saved Robot from them, but they probably aren't harmful. They must have thought we were attacking them. There could be others like them down there. We don't have any reason to destroy them."

"Wait a minute," said the Doby. "Are all you humans like this?"

"Like what?" asked Will.

"You know," started the Doby. "*Monster* lovers?"

"I guess it's something my mom once showed me," said Will. "When I was a kid —"

"What do you mean 'when' you were a kid?" said Penny with a laugh.

"I mean — a *little* kid," said Will. "I used to like to play in a cave near our house. It was filled with all kinds of bats and rocks and bugs and worms. It was just like the inside of this asteroid. I could never catch a bat, but once I brought home a bunch of worms . . ."

"Yeah, I remember," said Penny. "We used to call you 'Slimy Robinson.'"

Will ignored his sister's jibe. "Anyway, I studied the worms for about a week. Pretty soon they started to die and I didn't know why. Mom was cleaning out my room one day and found them. She told me I was killing them by studying them. She explained that many creatures can't live outside their natural environment. Even humans can't live on other planets without some artificial environment that provides the right kind of atmosphere and other conditions. After that, I brought the worms back to the cave and set them free. Whenever I wanted to study them I went to the cave — kinda like going to their house instead of bringing them over to mine."

"You learned this from your ma?" asked the Doby.

"Sure," said Will. "And also from my dad and some of the teachers at school."

"Well," said the Doby, pausing with thought. "There *is* that colony of giant worms about ten miles north from here. Each one is about the size of your spaceship. And, of course, there are the waterbugs . . ."

Penny gulped at the thought of the gross creatures. "Water-bugs?" she asked, uncertain if she wanted to hear any more.

"Yup," said the Doby. "They're not so bad, though. They're only about as big as your Robot. I was actually startin' to get used to those slimy critters. Thought I might make me a saddle, throw it over one of their backs, and have me a real space rodeo one day."

"Well, I guess we'll have to come up with another way to get out of here," said Penny.

"Wait a minute, Penny," said Will. "Did you say that the ship's cameras were recording all the time we were searching the asteroid?"

"That's right," replied Penny. "I've got about six hours of disks to log."

"Which camera was recording the area where we entered the cavern?"

"Camera two," said Penny, pointing to one of the video monitors.

"Can we view that disk at high speed?"

"Sure," said Penny. "Just give me a second to cue it."

"What's the plan, Willy-boy?" asked the Doby as he hovered around Will and Penny at the video station.

"I'm just curious about something," said Will. "We know that we came in through a hole in the asteroid. We also know that we recorded our entry and landing on video —"

"Video ready for viewing," interrupted Penny. She then pressed a button on her keyboard. An image of the tunnel opening appeared on the screen.

"There it is!" exclaimed Will. "The tunnel opening. Now fast forward, Penny."

Penny followed Will's order and sped up the video. In a few

minutes, the tunnel opening vanished and was replaced by a cavern wall.

"Stop video," said Will. Penny froze the image.

"Now the tunnel is gone," said Will. "But it was there a minute ago. Robot, can you explain that?"

"An explanation would be theoretical at best, Will Robinson," replied the Robot. "The properties of the Joh'ellian dimension are still unknown to me."

"A theoretical explanation is better than none, Robot," said Penny.

"Very well," replied the Robot. "It is possible that we are witnessing a fluctuation in the space-time continuum of this asteroid. The tunnel may be existing at a point in this dimension in which reality is constantly changing its physical structure. I would suggest viewing the video further to see if the tunnel reappears."

"Running video," said Penny. Again everyone watched as the image of the tunnel slowly appeared again. A few minutes later the tunnel vanished yet again.

Penny stopped the video. "This is where we were when we returned to the spaceship," she said. "No tunnel."

"An analysis of the time lapse between the tunnel's appearance is approximately once every ninety minutes," said the Robot.

"Great!" said Will with glee. "All we have to do is wait for the next time the tunnel appears, then blast off and get out of here."

"Caution, Will Robinson," said the Robot.

"What's wrong, Robot?" asked Will.

"Since our sensors cannot be trusted in this dimension we have no way of knowing how stable the space-time continuum of the tunnel is," replied the Robot. "The tunnel could remain

76

open for as long as several minutes or as short as a microsecond."

"Are you reckonin' what I think yer reckonin', pardner?" asked the Doby.

"I am warning that if we try to pass through the tunnel at its next appearance it may close up sooner than we expect."

"And if it does —?" asked the Doby.

"I know the answer to that," said Penny. "If it does, we could end up being trapped inside solid rock!"

19
Stone

Seconds passed. Minutes . . . an hour . . . then more.
Will had ordered everyone to their blastoff stations and
now the small crew of the *Jupiter 2* was waiting for the continuum tunnel to reappear. When that exact moment would
come, only the Robot could be sure. Everyone was scared.
They knew that there was just as much chance they would be
trapped inside solid rock as there was that they would escape
the asteroid.

"Tarnation," sighed the Doby. He was sitting in the seat beside Will. "How much longer you figger we have to wait for
this thing to appear?"

"We are in the last third of the ninety-minute interval," said
the Robot. "The space-time continuum should shift again in
two and one-half minutes," said the Robot.

"Turning on ship's ignition sequence," said Will, entering
the proper commands into Major West's ignition computer.
"Everybody strapped in?"

"Second-in-command and mascot strapped in for blastoff,"
replied Penny. She looked over and smiled at Blawp, who was
strapped into her flight seat.

"Science officer secured in stasis chamber," said the Robot after entering its specially designed compartment.

"Assistant pilot, A-OK!" said the Doby. "Let 'er rip, Willy-boy!"

"Ignition sequence activated," said Will. "If all goes smoothly we should be lifting off at the exact same time the continuum opens up."

"Ninety seconds to continuum shift," said the Robot. "And counting . . ."

"Will?" said Penny.

"Yeah?" replied Will.

"Whatever happens, I think you're a pretty good captain," said Penny.

"Thanks, Penny," said Will. "You're not a bad second-in-command, either."

"One minute to shift . . ." continued the Robot.

Will looked at the countdown meter on the ignition console. It was ticking off in perfect sync with the Robot. So far, so good. Still, Will crossed his fingers for luck.

"There it is!" said Penny as the Robot reached the end of the countdown. "I can see the tunnel on Monitor two now."

As she spoke the great engines of the *Jupiter 2* kicked in.

"We're lifting off right on schedule!" said Will as the ship rose up from the ground. Dust and debris from the floor of the asteroid's cavern created a cloud that was difficult to see through. However, with the help of the Doby he guided the *Jupiter 2* straight toward the opening of the tunnel.

"We're entering the tunnel now," said Will. "Activate thruster jets."

"Thruster jets activated," said the Doby, pressing a command on the control panel. At that, the ship lurched forward with power and entered the dark multidimensional tunnel.

"Robot, how soon until we reach the end of the tunnel?" asked Will as they traveled.

"At this rate of speed we should emerge from the asteroid in three minutes and five seconds," replied the Robot.

A second later, the Robot's domed head popped up in alert. "Warning! Warning!" it said. "Space-time continuum destabilizing! Space-time continuum destabilizing!"

"Will, I'm losing images of the tunnel on the monitors!" exclaimed Penny.

The tunnel was vanishing right before their eyes. Not only that, but parts of the ship seemed to be disappearing as well.

"I'm increasing ship's speed!" said Will. But as he reached forward for the controls he saw that they were now made of solid rock!

"Danger! Danger!" alerted the Robot. "The physical matter inside the spaceship is now melding with the physical matter of the continuum! In a few more seconds we will be —"

Suddenly, the Robot was quiet. Will turned around and saw that the Robot had been completely transformed into solid rock. Looking further around he saw that Penny, the Blawp, and most of the spaceship had also turned into stone. The sight was startling. Bright, shiny equipment had become charcoal-colored masses of granite and mica. Penny and the Blawp, once flesh and blood, were now ashen statues frozen in position.

Despite his shock, and with his heart pounding, he continued to try to speed up the spaceship. But gradually he found it harder and harder to move his hands. When he looked down he saw why. They had turned to stone, just like everything else. Now he was becoming part of the space-time continuum, too.

Suddenly, everything began to spin around him. He felt the rest of his body beginning to turn to stone. All was lost, he thought to himself. He and the others would be trapped inside a grave of stone forever.

It was the last thought he had before blacking out.

20
Mystery

"Awake, Will Robinson," came the voice of the Protector. "All is well."

Will opened his eyes. The first thing he saw was the Doby floating in front of him.

"Doby, is that you?" asked Will weakly.

"Have no fear," replied the Doby, speaking in the deep, majestic voice of the Protector. "It is I."

Will looked around. He was no longer made of stone, nor was the ship, the Robot, or Penny. Through the viewport he could see the blackness of space. That meant they were no longer inside the asteroid.

"Penny?" asked Will. "You all right?"

"I think so," said Penny, stirring in her seat.

"Who are you?" Will asked the Doby. "How did we get here?"

"I am the one you know as the Doby," replied the little man. "But I am also the one you know as the Protector."

In an instant, the Doby vanished into thin air. A second later, he appeared on the other side of the viewscreen, in outer space, transformed into the huge, ugly face of the Protector.

"I don't understand," said Will. "How did we get here?"

"It is I who returned you to this spot," explained the Protector. "Just as it was I who sent you into the asteroid. It was I, in the guise of the bat-creature, who challenged you in the cavern. And it was I, in the disguise of the Doby, using a voice I hoped would make you trust me, who rescued you from the rock monsters."

"Why?" asked Will.

"Call it a test, if you will," said the Doby. "You asked me to believe the words of your father; to believe him when he said that you meant us no harm. It is the children of any society who reflect the true teachings of their elders. If I could see that you were true and virtuous children, then I could believe your elders."

"You mean you were just testing us in that asteroid?" asked Penny. "You scared us to death just to see how we would react?"

"That is true," said the Protector. "I was impressed with your willingness to sacrifice yourself in order to rescue your family. I was even more impressed when you refused to destroy the living creatures inside the asteroid even though it could have meant your freedom. But, most of all, I was impressed with the way you both helped each other to survive the perils I lay in your path. Never did you utter words of disagreement or hostility. Your elders have taught you well, Will and Penny Robinson. I will return them to you now."

Within a few seconds Professor Robinson and Mrs. Robinson appeared from out of nowhere, back in the exact same spot Will and Penny had last seen them.

"Dad! Mom!" the children cried out as they ran to embrace their parents.

Next, Major West, Judy, and Dr. Smith all reappeared.

"Your children have proved your race to be a good and honorable one, John Robinson," said the Protector, after giving them a little time for a reunion. "There is no longer any need to destroy you. I will return you now to a place far outside the Ring of Joh'el. But because we wish to remain unknown to outsiders, you will have no memory of me or this experience. Begone!"

The *Jupiter* had been flying at a normal speed, aimless in its course. Will had locked himself in his cabin and was analyzing and reanalyzing some star-charts he had put together when Major West's voice came over the loudspeaker.

"Will, get up here to the control deck, pronto."

Will hurried topside where his father and Major West were looking at some star-chart data that was coming over the main computer.

"What do you know about this, Will?" asked Professor Robinson, indicating the constellation that appeared on the navigation computer monitor. It was filed under the name Electric Guitar.

"My Quadrant X star map!" said Will. "I thought I lost it. How did it get up here?"

"You don't know?" asked Major West. "Someone obviously put your disk into the computer and ran a vector analysis on it. Although I don't know why. We're probably light-years away from anything that looks like that constellation."

"That's strange," said Will. "Who would do that?"

"You're *sure* it wasn't you, Will?" asked Will's dad.

"Positive," said Will. "I mean it!"

"Will —" said Professor Robinson, sounding doubtful.

"He's telling the truth, John," said Major West. "I've been here the whole time since my shift started. There was nothing in the disk drive when I started. It's almost as if it appeared out of nowhere."

"That *is* mysterious," said Professor Robinson. "Robot, have we passed through any kind of multidimensional phase anomaly? Anything that might have resulted in the appearance of Will's disk in the computer?"

The Robot checked its sensors. "Negative, Professor Robinson," it replied. "All space and time is normal."

Professor Robinson shrugged. "I guess it's a mystery, then."

Will nodded. It *was* a mystery. The kind of mystery that can only happen amid the countless unmapped stars of outer space.